Chinese Americans

Dale Anderson

Curriculum Consultant: Michael Koren,
Social Studies Teacher, Maple Dale School, Fox Point, Wisconsin

WORLD ALMANAC® LIBRARY

To the Chinese Americans who immigrated to the United States and their descendants, in tribute to their perseverance and achievements in the face of mighty obstacles, and especially to Heidi.

Please visit our web site at: www.garethstevens.com
For a free color catalog describing World Almanac® Library's list of high-quality books and multimedia programs, call 1-800-848-2928 (USA) or 1-800-387-3178 (Canada). World Almanac® Library's fax: (414) 332-3567.

Library of Congress Cataloging-in-Publication Data

Anderson, Dale, 1953-
    Chinese Americans / by Dale Anderson.
        p. cm. – (World Almanac Library of American immigration)
    Includes bibliographical references and index.
    ISBN-10: 0-8368-7308-4 – ISBN-13: 978-0-8368-7308-5 (lib. bdg.)
    ISBN-10: 0-8368-7321-1 – ISBN-13: 978-0-8368-7321-4 (softcover)
    1. Chinese Americans–History–Juvenile literature.   2. Chinese Americans–
Social conditions–Juvenile literature.   3. Immigrants–United States–History–
Juvenile literature.   4. China–Emigration and immigration–History–Juvenile
Literature.   5. United States–Emigration and immigration–History–Juvenile
literature. I. Title. II. Series.
    E184.C5A55   2007
    973'.004951–dc22   2006005640

First published in 2007 by
World Almanac® Library
A member of the WRC Media Family of Companies
330 West Olive Street, Suite 100
Milwaukee, WI 53212, USA

Produced by Discovery Books
Editors: Jacqueline Gorman and Clare Weaver
Designer and page production: Sabine Beaupré
Photo researcher: Rachel Tisdale
Maps and diagrams: Stefan Chabluk
Consultant: Lorraine Dong
World Almanac® Library editorial direction: Mark J. Sachner
World Almanac® Library editor: Barbara Kiely Miller
World Almanac® Library art direction: Tammy West
World Almanac® Library production: Jessica Morris

Picture credits: CORBIS: /Reuters 17: /Bettmann 33; /Mark Peterson 38; /Owen Franken
39; Chris Fairclough/Chris Fairclough Worldwide Ltd: 43; Getty Images: /J. Emilio Flores
cover, 42; /Andrea Chu/Taxi 5; /Hulton Archive 7; /Jack Wilkes/Time & Life Pictures 8;
/Dylan Martinez/AFP 9; /Mansell/Time Life Pictures 12; /Hulton Archive 22; /Historic
Photo Archive 28; /FPG title page, 30; /Henry Guttmann 31; /Spencer Platt 35; /Ernst
Haas 37; The Granger Collection, New York: 19; Library of Congress: /George R. Lawrence
Co. 15; /T. de Thulstrop 25; /George Grantham Bain Collection 27; San Francisco History
Center/San Francisco Public Library: 16; TopFoto: /Lou Dematteis/The Image Works 21.

Printed in the United States of America

1 2 3 4 5 6 7 8 9 10 09 08 07 06

Contents

Front cover: Members of the Chinese American community take part in Chinese New Year celebrations in Chinatown, Los Angeles, California.

Title page: Young Chinese American schoolchildren pose for a school photograph in San Francisco's Chinatown, in the early 1900s.

Introduction

The United States has often been called "a nation of immigrants." With the exception of Native Americans—who have inhabited North America for thousands of years—all Americans can trace their roots to other parts of the world.

Immigration is not a thing of the past. More than seventy million people came to the United States between 1820 and 2005. One-fifth of that total—about fourteen million people—immigrated since the start of 1990. Overall, more people have immigrated permanently to the United States than to any other single nation.

Push and Pull

Historians write of the "push" and "pull" factors that lead people to emigrate. "Push" factors are the conditions in the homeland that convince people to leave. Many immigrants to the United States were—and still are—fleeing persecution or poverty. "Pull" factors are those that attract people to settle in another country. The dream of freedom or jobs or both continues to pull immigrants to the United States. People from many countries around the world view the United States as a place of opportunity.

Building a Nation

Immigrants to the United States have not always found what they expected. People worked long hours for little pay, often doing jobs that others did not want to do. Many groups also endured prejudice.

In spite of these challenges, immigrants and their children built the United States of America, from its

"My grandfather came to this country from China nearly a century ago and worked as a servant. Now I serve as governor just one mile from where my grandfather worked. It took our family one hundred years to travel that mile. It was a voyage we could only make in America."

Washington Governor Gary Locke, who in 1996 became the first Chinese American to be elected governor of a U.S. state

farms, railroads, and computer industries to its beliefs and traditions. They have enriched American life with their culture and ideas. Although they honor their heritage, most immigrants and their descendants are proud to call themselves Americans first and foremost.

The Chinese American Contribution

Nearly two million Chinese immigrants have come to the United States from China, Taiwan, and Hong Kong in four distinct waves of immigration. The first wave lasted from 1850 to 1882. Racial prejudice led the U.S. government to limit Chinese immigration in 1882, so the second wave, over the next fifty years, included fewer than one hundred thousand people. The 1940s saw some loosening of those limits and launched the third wave. A new immigration law was passed in 1965, opening the door to Chinese immigrants wider and beginning the fourth wave. In 2000, more than 2.7 million Chinese Americans lived in the United States.

Chinese American workers played a major role in building western railroads in the late 1800s. Chinatowns in San Francisco, California; New York City; and other cities have provided homes and workplaces to Chinese Americans. They also attract visitors from other groups of Americans as well as foreign tourists. Chinese Americans have set up successful companies and contributed to U.S. cultural life, and Chinese food has become a staple in the U.S.

▼ The entrance to Chinatown in San Francisco.

CHAPTER 1

Life in the Homeland

Chinese immigration to the United States has taken place over a period of more than 150 years. During that time, conditions in China changed dramatically. Those circumstances—along with U.S. laws—influenced why and when people moved from China to the United States. Understanding life in China at different times helps build an understanding of Chinese immigration.

China in the Middle 1800s

In the middle 1800s, the vast majority of Chinese people were farmers who worked on land owned by wealthy landowners. They lived in small homes with large families, scratching out a living. They had little control over their own lives.

Earlier, in the 1600s, European countries had sent traders to China to buy tea, porcelain, silk, and other valuable goods. European leaders noticed in the 1800s that the power of China's emperors was declining, and the Europeans began to take economic control over different areas of China. Some Chinese launched a revolt called

◀ This map shows China's provinces and neighboring countries today.

▲ Chinese workers operating by foot a huge irrigation wheel in a painting of 1811. Many Chinese laborers worked under similar harsh conditions at this time.

"How can we live on six baskets of rice which were paid twice a year for my father's duty as a night watch-man? Sometimes the peasants have a poor crop [and] then we go hungry. . . . Sometimes we went hungry for days. My mother and me would go over the harvested rice fields of the peasants to pick the grains they [had] dropped."

Unnamed Chinese man describing life in China in the middle 1800s

the Boxer Rebellion against the foreigners, but European soldiers defeated them.

China's farmers had no way to break out of their poverty and harsh lives if they remained in China. Bloody rebellions against the Europeans simply made their lives worse. By the 1850s, tens of thousands of farmers, especially from southeastern China, decided to leave the country for a better life. Some went to other countries, but many formed the first wave of Chinese immigration to the United States.

China in the Early 1900s

By the early 1900s, the Chinese empire had collapsed, and a new Republic of China was formed, with revolutionary Sun Yat-sen as its first president. He tried to modernize and limit foreign control of China. People in the southeast were still mainly poor farmers, however, and many wanted to leave, leading to the second wave of Chinese immigration.

In the late 1920s, after Sun Yat-sen's death, Chiang Kai-shek became China's military and political leader. Meanwhile, a young revolutionary named Mao Zedong and others formed the Chinese Communist Party. Mao vowed to change the Chinese economy and society. He gathered supporters and formed an army that fought Chiang's forces. This civil war was interrupted in the 1930s, when Japan invaded China. Chiang's and Mao's armies both fought the Japanese, in an effort that eventually became part of World War II. Japan surrendered in 1945 and its armies left China. Civil war then broke out again and lasted until 1949, when Mao won. Mao and the communists ruled the country's mainland, called the People's Republic of China. Chiang and his followers fled to the island of Taiwan. The People's Republic of China and Taiwan (as the Republic of China) remain separate today.

The Chinese civil war and World War II had some effect on Chinese immigration to the United States. During World War II, China and the United States were allied against Japan, which led U.S. leaders to lift some of the limits placed on Chinese immigration. These changes caused a brief, small jump in immigration, and the Chinese who came then formed the third wave.

The Two Chinas

From 1949 to the early 1980s, the communist government strictly controlled all aspects of life on the mainland. People did not enjoy freedom of speech or religion. The economy was poor. People lived in crowded housing, had shortages of food, and enjoyed few luxuries such as cars or televisions. Along with new, less strict U.S. immigration laws, those conditions prompted many thousands to leave China for the United States, producing the fourth (and by far the largest) wave of Chinese immigration.

Life in Taiwan was not very free either. Chiang Kai-shek controlled Taiwan, and people lived in fear that they would be accused of supporting the communists. However, Chiang Kai-shek took steps to build the economy, so Taiwan prospered. Still, some educated Taiwanese disliked the lack of freedom, causing many to emigrate to the United States.

Recent Changes in the People's Republic of China

In the 1980s, new leaders reformed China's economy and opened trade with the outside world. This led to higher wages for many Chinese. Goods such as clothing, furniture, televisions, and cars became more plentiful, and the Chinese enjoyed a better lifestyle. Many, though, remained frustrated over the lack of political freedom, and others found that they were not part of the growing prosperity. Some began to look for work in other countries. For these reasons, the fourth wave of immigration continues today.

This fourth wave of immigration was boosted by the changing status of Hong Kong. The British had taken control of this city in southeastern China in the 1800s because it had an excellent harbor. In the late 1900s, Hong Kong thrived as a center of manufacturing, banking, and shipping. Under British rule, the people of Hong Kong enjoyed more prosperity and freedom than those in communist China, and some people fled China for Hong Kong, using it as a stepping stone to reach the United States. In 1984, however,

▶ Members of the Chinese Armed Forces stand at attention under the Chinese and British flags during the ceremony marking the handover of Hong Kong to China in July 1997.

> "We [were] in Hong Kong a little over three years. . . . Things began to happen, . . . and we thought Hong Kong was threatened. . . . We said, 'If it took us all that trouble to get out of the country to go to Hong Kong, if there is the remotest chance of their taking over Hong Kong, we're going to leave.' . . . We had our little girl by then, and thinking of the future of the children, we don't want anything like what we experienced ever to happen to them."
>
> *Betty Chu, who left China for Hong Kong in 1966 and came to the United States in 1969*

Britain agreed to hand Hong Kong over to China in 1997. Thousands of people left the city before the handover, fearing that communist rule would cut into their prosperity and freedom. Others left after the handover. These people are part of the fourth wave of Chinese immigration as well.

Chinese Culture

China has seen many changes in the last 150 years, especially after the communist victory in 1949. Still, some customs and ideas are deeply rooted in Chinese life and have been brought to the United States by Chinese Americans.

The writings of the philosopher Confucius, who lived in China in about 500 B.C., helped shape Chinese culture and society. Confucius stressed the need for filial piety—a deep respect that children showed for their parents, especially their father. Children showed this respect by obeying their fathers, even when they had become adults. Fathers, in turn, led the family in performing rituals that honored their ancestors. Through these rituals, fathers hoped to please the ancestors' spirits, who would help bring good fortune to the family.

Sons were more highly valued in China than daughters. It was through male children that a father could continue his family line—which ensured that future generations would perform rituals for him, just as he had done for his ancestors. Females had lower social standing than males. The followers of Confucius quoted him as saying that women should show "obedience to the father when yet unmarried, obedience to the husband when married, and obedience to the sons when widowed."

Marriages in China were typically arranged by families, instead of being matches based on the love between a man and woman. A bride moved into her husband's home. She was expected to work hard and obey her father-in-law and mother-in-law. It was hoped that she would have many children—especially sons. Wives were often not even seen outside the home.

Strong ties bound family members together. In a farming family, everyone was expected to help work the land and contribute to the family's success. Family members hid any problems from people outside the family. If someone in the family made a mistake, it brought shame on the whole family. To avoid that shame, children learned very early to behave themselves.

China had two main religions. Taoism emphasized the importance of balance between reason and emotion and the value of keeping in touch with the spirits of nature. Buddhism, brought to China from India, taught that putting too much focus on material things—homes, possessions, food—leads to suffering because eventually those things would be lost. Buddhist teachers told people to focus on spiritual growth.

China has had a long and impressive history. The Chinese invented paper, printing, gunpowder, paper money, and many other useful products. They perfected the crafts of making silk, porcelain, and other fine goods. Their art, literature, and philosophy included brilliant works. The Chinese were proud of these achievements, and many Americans and Europeans admired them. By the 1800s and 1900s, however, Western nations and technology had become more powerful, and many Westerners did not understand the principles on which Chinese culture was based. For these reasons, many in the United States viewed the Chinese as backward and saw their own culture as superior. These attitudes often led to harsh treatment of the Chinese immigrants who came to the United States.

Different Groups and Languages

China is a huge country, and all Chinese do not come from the same ethnic group. People in different regions have different origins, and they do not always treat those from other groups fairly. They also speak different dialects, which means they cannot always communicate with each other. Most of those who have emigrated from China to the United States came from the province of Guangdong. They are called Cantonese after Canton, the old name for the major city in the region (now called Guangzhou). In recent years, growing numbers of people—called Fujianese—have come from the province of Fujian.

CHAPTER 2

Emigration

The people who made up the four waves of Chinese immigration faced different conditions at home. As a result, they generally left China for different reasons. They also differed from each other in terms of gender, age, background, and education, and in terms of what they were looking for by emigrating.

The Men of the First Wave

The first Chinese immigrants left their homeland between 1850 and 1882. Today, historians call them "sojourners" because they did not intend to leave China permanently but planned to work in the United States for a year or two, earning as much money as possible. Then they planned to return to China to buy their own land. About half of these travelers did eventually go back to China, but the rest stayed.

Because they were sojourners, the overwhelming majority of these immigrants were men. By 1880, Chinese immigrant males outnumbered females by almost twenty-five to one. About half the men were single, but even married men did not bring their families because they did not think they would be in the United States for long. Chinese traditions also played a role in the decision to leave their wives in

◄ A Chinese vendor stands next to eggs, vegetables, and spices for sale at a store in San Francisco's Chinatown, 1890.

China. Chinese women rarely left their homes, even to walk in their villages. A journey across the ocean would have been highly unusual.

Most of the Cantonese farmers who came to the United States were poor. As a result, many did not have the money to pay for passage across the Pacific Ocean. A few of them raised the money from family members, but the great majority borrowed the money for the passage, figuring that they could repay the loans from their earnings. Some agreed to labor contracts in which businessmen paid their passage and guaranteed them a job for a few years. These businessmen then sold the laborers' services to companies in the United States, making a profit by paying the workers less than they received.

Limiting Chinese Immigration

Companies in the United States paid the first wave of Chinese immigrants less than they paid white workers. This cheaper labor made many white workers angry because they felt that the Chinese were taking jobs away from them, and they began to pressure the government to limit Chinese immigration. That pressure continued and grew throughout the 1870s.

Finally, in 1882, Congress passed the Chinese Exclusion Act, which barred Chinese laborers—the vast majority of Chinese immigrants—from entering the United States. It allowed merchants, students, and teachers to enter, but not ordinary working men. This law marked the first time in U.S. history that the nation banned immigration from a particular country. The law also barred most Chinese women from entering. No single women could come—only wives—but the law allowed only wives whose husbands were permitted to immigrate.

The Chinese Exclusion Act set this ban on Chinese immigration for ten years. It was renewed for another ten years in 1892 by the Geary Act and then made permanent in 1904. Together, these laws cut Chinese immigration to a relative trickle.

"[The] present Chinese invasion [is] pernicious and should be discouraged. Our experience in dealing with the weaker races—the Negroes and Indians . . . —is not encouraging. . . . I would consider with favor any suitable measures to discourage the Chinese from coming to our shores."

President Rutherford B. Hayes, discussing Chinese immigration in 1879

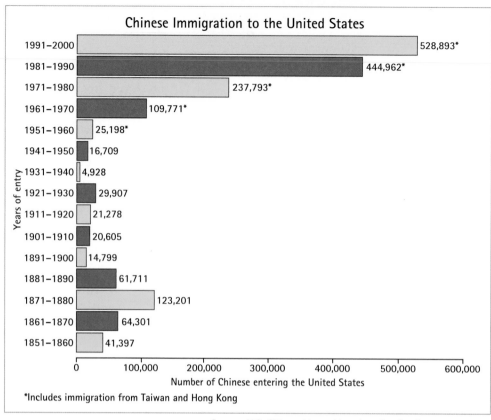

Chinese Immigration to the United States

Years of entry	Number
1991–2000	528,893*
1981–1990	444,962*
1971–1980	237,793*
1961–1970	109,771*
1951–1960	25,198*
1941–1950	16,709
1931–1940	4,928
1921–1930	29,907
1911–1920	21,278
1901–1910	20,605
1891–1900	14,799
1881–1890	61,711
1871–1880	123,201
1861–1870	64,301
1851–1860	41,397

Number of Chinese entering the United States

*Includes immigration from Taiwan and Hong Kong

Source: U.S. Citizenship and Immigration Services, 1851–2000

▲ This chart shows the numbers of Chinese immigrants entering the United States in ten-year periods from 1851–2000.

"In the beginning my father came in as a laborer. But the 1906 earthquake came along and destroyed all those immigration [records]. So that was a big chance for a lot of Chinese. They forged themselves certificates saying they were born in this country, and then when the time came, they could go back to China and bring back four or five sons, just like that!"

Hay Ming Lee, describing immigration in the second wave

Wives and "Paper Sons"

The second wave of Chinese immigration began with the small number of merchants, students, and their wives who were allowed to enter after the Exclusion Act was passed. The biggest number of people in the second wave came as the result of a dramatic event in the United States. In 1906, a terrible earthquake shook San Francisco. The quake destroyed many buildings, including those holding government records about births and immigrant arrivals. As a result, many Chinese in California could claim that they had been born in the United States. According to the Fourteenth Amendment to the Constitution, approved in 1868, that fact

▶ This photograph shows the extent of damage from the 1906 San Francisco earthquake. The destruction of government records in the earthquake led to many Chinese claiming they had been born in the United States.

meant they were citizens. As citizens, they could bring their wives and children to the United States because the Exclusion Act did not apply to them.

The result was a sharp increase in Chinese immigration. Chinese men in the United States returned to China to find their wives, and from 1907 to 1924, about ten thousand Chinese women entered the United States. An even greater number of young men came. They are called "paper sons" because many were not truly the sons of the men who claimed to be their fathers. Chinese Americans who claimed to be citizens would return to China and declare that they had children born to them there. Then they could bring these children to the United States as family members. Some did bring back actual sons, but many brought over cousins, nephews, neighbors, or even complete strangers. Some Chinese families paid Chinese Americans to claim their male children as their own sons, thus giving those children a chance to come to the United States. Some men brought "paper daughters" as well.

Missionaries in China

A number of Westerners traveled to China in the 1800s and early 1900s. Some were businesspeople who worked in the profitable business of trading Chinese goods. Others were missionaries, many from the United States, who hoped to convert the Chinese to Christianity. They settled in the countryside, building churches and schools. By 1900, about one hundred thousand Chinese had adopted Christianity. Some of the missionaries and their children grew strongly attached to China and its people. Publisher Henry Luce and writer Pearl Buck were two of these missionary children.

Cracks in the Closed Door

Although the stream of wives and paper sons increased Chinese immigration from 1910 to 1920, laws still barred large numbers of Chinese from coming to the United States. Not until the 1930s and 1940s did U.S. attitudes toward the Chinese soften.

One cause for changing attitudes was the influence of Americans who liked China and the Chinese people. One of these was former missionary child Henry Luce, publisher of *Time* and *Life* magazines, which were influential publications. Another was novelist Pearl Buck (also a former missionary child), whose books portrayed Chinese farmers in positive ways. One of her books, *The Good Earth* (1931), became a best-seller and a Hollywood movie, helping promote favorable attitudes toward China and Chinese people.

▲ A group of Chinese war brides learning English at the Chinese Y.M.C.A. in San Francisco, 1948.

Even more important, however, was the change caused by World War II. The United States and China were allies in the war, and their alliance prompted changes in U.S. laws. In 1943, Congress passed the Magnuson Act, finally ending the exclusion of Chinese immigrants. Still, that law set a quota of only 105 Chinese immigrants each year.

After the war, other laws made it possible for even more Chinese immigrants to enter the country. The War Brides Act allowed U.S. soldiers to bring into the United States women from other countries whom they had married. About six thousand Chinese women who had married U.S. servicemen were brought to the United States. A large proportion of the women were the new wives of Chinese American soldiers. Laws passed in 1948 and 1953 allowed for the arrival of several thousand refugees fleeing the communist takeover in China, bringing about ten thousand Chinese into the country above the quota. In 1962, President John F. Kennedy signed a presidential order that allowed another fifteen thousand Chinese refugees to enter the United States.

These immigrants from the war and postwar years made up the third wave. They differed from the earliest immigrants in one major way—nearly nine of every ten Chinese immigrants during this period were female.

Leaving China in the Fourth Wave

The major change in Chinese immigration, however, did not come until 1965, when Congress passed a new immigration law. It set the quota for immigrants from China at twenty thousand a year. For the first time since 1882, large numbers of Chinese could enter the country. In 1986, other laws expanded Chinese immigration further by setting up separate quotas for mainland China and Taiwan of twenty thousand each and for Hong Kong at five thousand people per year. These laws spurred the large numbers of Chinese immigrants who make up the fourth wave.

This fourth wave consists of three distinct groups. The first is made up of highly educated and skilled people—doctors, engineers, teachers, and technicians. They typically come with their families and intend to stay. Many want the freedom found in the United States but not in China. The second group—made up of poorer and less educated people—are fleeing poverty and unemployment back home. The third group is comprised of Chinese from Taiwan, many of whom came to the United States as students in the 1960s. Disliking the rigid society that had been set up on Taiwan, the great majority stayed in the United States once they had earned their degrees.

Adopted Children

Since 1992, a few thousand Chinese children have left China each year after being adopted by parents in other countries. China supplies more adopted children than any other country. The average age of these children is eleven months, and more than nine of every ten are girls, reflecting the low regard in which daughters are held in Chinese culture. Chinese children adopted by U.S. citizens gain their parents' status as citizens as soon as they enter the country or when the adoption is final.

Arriving in the United States

T he experiences of those arriving in the United States at different times during the 150 years of Chinese immigration varied. Throughout the years, however, many immigrants were greeted with hostility and unfair treatment.

Seeking "Gold Mountain"

Poverty in China was not the only factor that led Chinese laborers to leave their homes for the United States in the early 1850s. The other was the promise of wealth in California. In 1848, gold was discovered in California, which prompted a huge movement of people seeking their fortune, called the "Gold Rush." Among the many thousands of people streaming to the area were more than twenty thousand Chinese immigrants who hoped to make their fortune in the land they called *gam saan,* or "Gold Mountain."

These early arrivals had to endure a difficult voyage across the Pacific Ocean crowded into the steerage section of a steamship. They lived in cramped quarters with little fresh air, bad food, and smelly conditions. On reaching San Francisco—where most landed—they were met by someone from one of the groups that earlier Chinese immigrants had set up. These greeters arranged a temporary place for the new arrivals to stay and gave them guidance on how to move to the gold fields.

The new arrivals took one important step before moving on to their destinations. They left directions for having their bodies shipped back to China for burial should they die. They feared that if they were buried in a strange land, their spirits would be restless.

The Paper Sons Reach U.S. Shores

The women and paper sons who came after the 1906 San Francisco earthquake had to pass through a new immigration station on

▶ Chinese boys awaiting medical examination at Angel Island immigration station in San Francisco Bay, 1910.

Angel Island in San Francisco Bay. Conditions there were poor. Women and girls were crowded into rooms holding twenty or thirty people, while as many as 170 men and boys were thrown together in other rooms. Beds were bunks or hammocks for those lucky enough not to have to sleep on the floor. Food, of poor quality, was given only in small amounts.

Even worse were the questions. Immigration officials had to approve the entry of each person. They knew that some of the young men trying to enter the country were not, in fact, the real sons of the Chinese Americans who claimed them. Thus, they questioned the arrivals closely, hoping to trap them into revealing their true family or admitting they were lying. The officials asked questions such as how many steps the family home had, where in the home they slept, and

Angel Island

The immigration station on Angel Island, in San Francisco Bay, was built in 1910 to process and record immigrants coming to the United States from Asia. Over the next thirty years, about 175,000 Chinese immigrants passed through the island. Treatment of immigrants there was harsher than on Ellis Island in New York City, the main immigration station in the east for handling immigrants from Europe. About one-third of immigrants passing through Angel Island were returned to their home countries, while only a small fraction of those who went through Ellis Island were sent back. The average stay of an immigrant on Angel Island was two to three weeks. In contrast, most immigrants passed through Ellis Island in only one day.

"Imprisoned in the wooden building day after day,

My freedom withheld; how can I bear to talk about it?

The days are long and the bottle constantly empty; my sad mood, even so, is not dispelled.

Nights are long, and the pillow cold; who can pity my loneliness?"

Poem written on the walls of a room in Angel Island by an unnamed Chinese immigrant being held there

what work their father did. Those who could not answer the questions satisfactorily were sent back to China. As word of these questions spread, the paper sons prepared by learning facts about their "fathers" during the ocean trip.

World War II and After

Conditions were less difficult for those who came from China immediately after World War II. War brides arrived by ship in large numbers to join their husbands or by plane alongside their husbands. What they did face, however, was an adjustment to a new way of life.

The refugees who entered the United States after the communist takeover of China found a relatively warm welcome. Some had been well-placed government officials or educated professionals. Still, this group also faced personal losses. Many had to leave behind family members, close friends, and personal belongings in the scramble to escape China.

Arriving in the Late Twentieth Century

The Chinese immigrants making up the fourth wave—those who came after 1965—typically flew to their new homeland and usually faced few problems entering the United States. Some were helped by the universities they would be attending or the companies they were coming to work for. Poorer immigrants were often welcomed by family members whom they were joining. As in the past, some immigrants faced prejudice, mistrust, and anger in their new cities, schools, and workplaces.

Many of these new immigrants followed the pattern called "chain migration." Immigration laws allow people with technical skills and family members of U.S. citizens to enter the country regardless of quotas. In this way, a Chinese student at a U.S. university could apply to stay after graduation on the basis of having special skills. He or she could then bring over a spouse and children. After five years, the former student could become a citizen and send for his or her parents. The new citizen could also bring in a brother or sister, who each started a new chain of immigration.

Illegal Entry

Since the 1980s, many Chinese people have come to the United States illegally. They come for the same reasons as other immigrants, in the hope of finding jobs and getting ahead. People called "snakeheads" organize the effort, collecting high fees from each immigrant. They charge not only for transportation but also for fake documents and for bribes to officials in China. Many immigrants come directly to the United States by boat, while others travel first to Mexico or Canada and then come over land. The extent of this illegal immigration is not clear, but probably numbers tens of thousands of Chinese each year.

"American students always picked on us, frightened us, made fun of us and laughed at our English. They broke our lockers, threw food on us in the cafeteria, said dirty words to us, pushed us on campus. Many times they shouted at me, 'Get out of here, you chink, go back to your country.' "

Christina Tien, who came to the United States as a child in the fourth wave

▼ Officials seize a boat smuggling about one hundred illegal Chinese immigrants in Half Moon Bay, California.

CHAPTER 4

Facing Prejudice

Limits on immigration made the lives of the first and second waves of Chinese Americans very difficult. They lived in a world of mostly men and faced the most brutal and violent anti-Chinese prejudice. They also worked under extremely harsh conditions in a wide variety of jobs. Despite all these problems and challenges, they began building the Chinese American community and creating institutions that are still part of Chinese American life today.

Mining for Gold

The Chinese immigrants who worked in California's gold fields in the early 1850s faced many obstacles. They generally arrived in the area after white prospectors got there, so most of the best sites had already been claimed. Still, they worked hard to try to find gold.

At first, they panned for gold, as the white miners had done. This method involved scooping up gravel in a pan, adding water, and moving the pan to wash the lighter dirt away from the heavier gold, which would stay on the bottom of the pan. Chinese miners soon began to work together, building dams and

▶ Chinese workers panning for gold in California's goldfields, 1855.

water wheels—devices that made it more efficient to run water over the soil. In capturing the power of flowing water, they used technology that had long been used in China for growing rice but was less familiar in the United States.

Life in the gold fields was difficult. Merchants charged high prices for food, clothing, and other supplies. Mining camps were often lawless, and Chinese miners were often attacked and robbed. Despite these challenges, they persevered.

Moving to Other Work

By the middle 1860s, most of California's gold had been taken. Mining work was still available elsewhere in the west, however, and by 1870, about seventeen thousand Chinese Americans worked as miners in several states and territories west of the Rocky Mountains. Some staked their own claims and tried to find gold using the methods that had been used in California. Others found work as laborers for large companies that mined gold, silver, or other metals.

"They prove nearly equal to white men in the amount of labor they perform, and are much more reliable. No danger of strikes among them. We are training them to all kinds of labor: blasting, driving horses, handling rock as well as pick and shovel."

Charles Crocker, who supervised the building of the Central Pacific Railroad in the 1860s, describing the Chinese American workers under him

Thousands of Chinese laborers also began working to build railroads. In the 1860s, Congress gave two railroad companies the right to build a rail line from Nebraska to California. The Central Pacific Railroad was in charge of building the western part of this line, but it could not find enough men to do the work. In 1865, Charles Crocker, who was in charge of the work, decided to hire Chinese immigrants to build the railroad.

Over the next four years, twelve thousand Chinese immigrants toiled away in this effort. Their work was grueling. They had to clear the land, break rocks, dig tunnels, build bridges, and lay tracks—all using nothing more than pickaxes, shovels, carts, and occasionally small amounts of dynamite. They worked in all weather conditions, including the snowy and cold winters that hit the mountains.

They toiled twelve hours a day, six days a week, for as little as $26 (about $300 today) a month. This was two-thirds of what the railroad paid whites for the same work. The work was dangerous as well: About 1,200 Chinese American workers died in the effort.

After the Central Pacific was finished in 1869, Chinese laborers went on to build other railroads in the west and the south. Others moved into fishing and fish processing in several areas of the west coast from California to Washington. Some went to Louisiana, where they joined the shrimp industry.

Working on Farms

Chinese Americans also became farm workers. By 1886, nine in ten California farm workers were Chinese, and they helped build the state's farm economy. The deltas of the Sacramento and San Joaquin Rivers in central California were similar to deltas in southeastern China. Chinese Americans used techniques they had learned at home to drain the marshy deltas and turn them into productive farmland. One government official noted that the work made the land twenty-five times more valuable than it had been before.

Some Chinese Americans wished to become farm owners. They faced obstacles, however, because California and other western states passed laws that blocked Asians from owning land. To work around these laws, Chinese Americans leased, or rented, land from white landowners. They shared with the landowner the profits gained from selling the crops.

Attacks on Chinese Americans

Chinese immigrants briefly enjoyed good relations with white Americans in the early 1850s. Lai Chun-Cheun, a Chinese American merchant in San Francisco, remembered, "The people of [China] were received like guests . . . [and] greeted with favor." The welcome did not last long. In 1852, California passed a state law that put a tax of $3 (about $70 today) per month on land mined for gold by Chinese miners. White miners did not have to pay this tax.

White U.S. workers grew increasingly hostile toward the Chinese. This attitude was shown in the growing pressure on Congress to pass a law banning immigration from China. Even worse, whites sometimes physically attacked Chinese Americans. The first major attack took place in 1871 in Los Angeles, after the accidental shooting of a white man by a Chinese. A white mob went on a rampage

▲ This painting shows the attack on Chinese miners at Rock Springs, Wyoming, 1885.

and killed nineteen Chinese Americans. Nine years later, an anti-Chinese riot in Denver, Colorado resulted in the death of one Chinese American, the beating of several more, and the destruction of dozens of Chinese homes. In 1885, white miners attacked Chinese miners in Rock Springs, Wyoming. When the fight was over, twenty-eight Chinese Americans were dead, several more were injured, and many were forced to leave the town. Other outbreaks took place in many other western states and territories where Chinese Americans had settled.

In 1868, the U.S. government had signed a treaty with China promising to protect Chinese Americans, but the government did little over the years to stop the attacks or punish those who carried them out. Chinese Americans protested, but with no results. Huie Kin, who lived in San Francisco in the 1870s, later recalled how difficult life was for Chinese Americans in this period: "We were simply terrified; we kept indoors after dark for fear of being shot in the back. Children spit upon us as we passed by and called us rats."

Personal Problems

Chinese immigrant men also lived with intense loneliness. Some brought or sent for their wives, but the Exclusion Act made that impossible for most of them. Another law made their lives even more difficult. In 1888, the Scott Act barred Chinese laborers who left the United States from entering the country again. This meant that men could no longer go home to China to visit their families

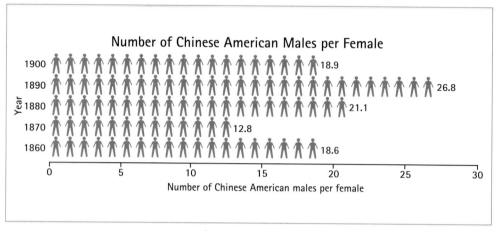

Number of Chinese American Males per Female

Year	
1900	18.9
1890	26.8
1880	21.1
1870	12.8
1860	18.6

Number of Chinese American males per female

▲ This chart shows the overwhelming predominance of males in the Chinese American community in the years 1860 to 1900.

"My Beloved Wife: It has been several autumns now since your dull husband left you for a far remote alien land. . . . Yesterday I received another of your letters. I could not keep tears from running down my cheeks when thinking about the miserable and needy circumstances of our home, and thinking back to the time of our separation. . . . Because I can get no gold, I am detained in this secluded corner of a strange land."

Unnamed Chinese immigrant, writing back to his wife in China in an unfinished letter

and return to the United States to work. Some twenty thousand Chinese American men were stranded in China when the law was passed, unable to return to the United States. Others decided to go back to China rather than continue their lonely and difficult lives.

The absence of families, the unfair treatment, and the harsh laws had an effect on the size of the Chinese community in the United States. In 1890, 107,488 Chinese lived in the United States. The deaths of some Chinese cut into these numbers, as did the decision by many to return to China. By 1910, the number of Chinese Americans had fallen to slightly more than 71,000.

Settling in Cities

From the start, many Chinese immigrants settled in cities. San Francisco had the most Chinese Americans. In 1870, the city was home to about twelve thousand of them, nearly one of every six Chinese Americans in the United States. Other major settlements were the California cities of Sacramento, Stockton, and Los Angeles. By the 1880s,

Chinese American communities had also arisen in other western cities such as Seattle and Tacoma in Washington and Portland, Oregon. By 1910, just about half of all Chinese Americans lived in cities.

In each city, Chinese Americans were crowded into small areas called "Chinatowns." While other immigrant groups also tended to settle near each other, Chinatowns were different from other ethnic neighborhoods. New York City's "Little Italy" overlapped with Jewish neighborhoods, and Chicago's immigrant neighborhoods included Italians, Poles, Lithuanians, and other groups. Chinatowns, however, were almost exclusively Chinese. The prejudice of whites

A Different Experience: The Chinese in Hawaii

Life was different for the Chinese living in Hawaii. The islands included many different groups, including immigrants from China, Japan, the Philippines, and Europe as well as whites and native-born Hawaiians. Over time, many of the immigrants developed good relations with people from other groups. One Hawaiian-born Chinese American came to a California university in the 1920s and was shocked when other students she met treated her as being different. "I did not stop to think of myself as being distinctly a Chinese and of my friends as being . . . some other nationality," she wrote.

▲ A photograph of the Hawaiian Chinese American baseball team in the early 1900s.

▲ Chinese men gather in a Chinese-owned store in Portland, Oregon, 1890.

forced the Chinese to live in these isolated areas where they owned the businesses, ran the shops, and worked in the factories.

Factory work was one attraction of city life. San Francisco factories made shoes, boots, cigars, and clothing. Many of these factories were in Chinatown, and Chinese Americans made up half the city's manufacturing workers. Their jobs dried up, however, when factories closed because products made in San Francisco could be made less expensively on the east coast. Also, white workers convinced businesses not to hire Chinese workers.

A new institution arose as a result: the Chinese laundry. Chinese Americans could open a laundry with relatively little money, and they did not have to work for someone else. The laundries started in Chinatowns but soon moved beyond those boundaries as owners placed their shops in the middle of non-Chinese neighborhoods to get business.

Still, the owners did not have to learn English but could communicate with their customers using signs or pictures. By 1900, one of every four Chinese American workers was employed in laundries.

Some Chinese Americans saved enough money to open stores. The shops, which sold Chinese food, books, and other products, became gathering places for the mostly male Chinese American community. Men would come at night after work to talk, read newspapers from China, play games, or sing traditional songs. These hours were welcome breaks from the long hours of work and the nights of loneliness.

Tying Chinese Americans Together

Chinese Americans formed different groups to unite them. Clan groups linked together all the people who shared the same name—the Lees or the Wongs, for instance. Another set of groups, called district associations, included all the clans that had come from the same district in China. There were six district associations, and they came to be called the Six Companies.

The Six Companies, which arose in San Francisco in about 1862, helped keep order in the Chinese American community. Officials of the companies met immigrants when they arrived and helped them complete the necessary paperwork. They settled arguments between members and worked to convince Chinese Americans to obey U.S. laws and the standards of good behavior in Chinatown. The Six Companies provided food and shelter to those who did not have a job and helped them find work. They cared for those who were sick and carried out funeral arrangements for those who died. They also tried to push government officials to treat Chinese Americans better.

The Tongs and Crime

Other groups formed in the Chinese American community as well. Those called tongs were criminal organizations. The tongs ran gambling clubs, houses of prostitution, and opium dens. (Opium is a highly addictive drug that comes from the poppy flower. It was introduced into China by the British.) The tongs were able to carry out their activities by paying bribes to police officials to leave them alone. Tong activities helped give Chinatowns a reputation for being centers of crime.

In 1882, in the face of the Exclusion Act, the Six Companies formally joined into a group called the Chinese Consolidated Benevolent Association (CCBA). CCBAs also formed in other cities that had large numbers of Chinese Americans.

The Early 1900s to 1930

In the first decades of the twentieth century, Chinese American life changed. The community was still overwhelmingly male, but less so. In 1910, more than 90 percent of all Chinese Americans were males. By 1930, however, males accounted for only 80 percent, and their share of the population kept falling. The population was younger, too, with more children. In 1900, only 3 percent of all Chinese Americans were children under age fourteen. By 1930, that share had risen to 20 percent.

The work that Chinese Americans did changed as well. Work on mines and railroads had ended, and Chinese Americans had been pushed off California's farms. By 1920, they accounted for only 1 percent of California's farm workers. By 1930, nearly three-quarters of all Chinese Americans lived in cities. The majority, one Chinese American wrote, found work in one of four kinds of businesses: "chop suey and chow mein restaurants, Chinese art and gift shops, native grocery stores that sell foodstuffs imported from China to the local Chinese communities, and Chinese laundries."

▲ Chinese American schoolchildren pose for a class photograph outside their school in Chinatown, San Francisco, in the early years of the twentieth century.

▶ A worker in a Chinese laundry, in 1935, wraps clothes in brown paper after they have been washed and ironed.

Most Chinese Americans were struggling to get by. Necessity forced women to work in family-owned stores, restaurants, and laundries. Children worked, too. One, whose family ran a laundry, remembered, "When I got to be eight or nine years old [my parents] showed me how to work the [irons] and I went from T-shirts and handkerchiefs to complicated things like shirts." Families often lived in rooms above or behind these businesses. Some had only one room that functioned as workplace by day and bedroom by night.

The presence of Chinese laundries in other neighborhoods made Chinese Americans more visible to other Americans. So did the promotion of Chinatowns as tourist attractions. In 1909, the CCBA published a book called *San Francisco's Chinatown* that tried to pull in visitors to the area's stores and restaurants. Tours were set up in San Francisco and in New York City, which had the country's second largest Chinese American community and the second largest Chinatown.

Despite growing contact, relations between Chinese and non-Chinese Americans remained distant. Some of the sights shown to tourists played on stereotypes about Chinese culture that were false, such as the idea that Chinese people ate rats. These ideas contributed to the view that Chinese Americans were different—an attitude that Chinese Americans felt keenly. They warned their children to be careful, saying, "Yes, legally you are Americans, but you will not be accepted. Look at your face—it is Chinese."

CHAPTER **5**

Building New Lives

The middle and late twentieth century saw the Chinese American community change in many ways, with many of those changes for the better. The Chinese American population grew as old immigration limits were finally lifted, and it became more evenly balanced between males and females and adults and children. Older Chinese Americans gained rights they had long been denied, and white U.S. citizens grew more accepting of Chinese Americans—though cases of prejudice and racial hatred still occurred. The makeup of the community changed as well, first with a shift to more members born in the United States and then, toward the end of the century, with a move back to more newly arrived immigrants. By the end of the 1990s, the Chinese American community was very different from what it had been in 1930, yet some similarities existed as well.

The Great Depression

The Great Depression of the 1930s hit the Chinese American community hard. In this economic collapse, millions in the United States lost their jobs and were forced to scrounge for food and shelter. Non-Chinese people had little extra money for laundering clothes or buying Chinese food—mainstay businesses of the Chinese American community. Chinese workers also lost their jobs, so there was less money to spend keeping Chinatown businesses afloat.

Businesses closed, and many Chinese families suffered. Some Chinese Americans accepted relief aid from the federal government, but they were a smaller percentage than the national average since many were too proud to take what they regarded as handouts. Others found the help they needed through the CCBA.

The tight job market in the United States led to a reverse migration. When well-educated young Chinese Americans—some of whom were trained as doctors or engineers—lost their jobs, they were not willing to return to Chinatowns to work as waiters. Instead, some returned to China to work there. These Chinese Americans, like their fathers and grandfathers decades before, were sojourners. They stayed in China for a few years and then returned to the United States when the U.S. economy improved.

The Impact of War on Chinese Americans

In 1931, the Japanese army seized Manchuria, a province of China, and Chinese Americans watched closely as tensions rose between Japan and China. Large-scale war broke out in 1937, when the Japanese tried to extend their control from Manchuria to the rest of China.

When Chinese officials came to the United States seeking U.S. support, Chinese Americans turned out in large numbers to cheer them. Despite the hardship of the Great Depression, they raised money to send to China to help in the war. Some young Chinese Americans joined the Chinese armed forces.

When the United States entered World War II by declaring war on Japan in late 1941, Chinese Americans took part in the war effort. Nearly one in five Chinese American males served in the U.S. armed forces, while

Chinese in the Movies in the 1930s

In the 1930s, two Chinese characters appeared in movies that were very popular with non-Chinese audiences. One was the evil genius Fu Manchu, the head of a criminal empire. The other was the clever detective Charlie Chan, who spoke in proverbs while he solved crimes. Both characters were played by white actors. Both perpetuated false and misleading stereotypes of Chinese people and culture, and they were bitterly regarded by Chinese Americans.

▲ A Chinese American woman working at a Californian defense plant in 1943.

> "In the 1940s for the first time Chinese were accepted by Americans as being friends because . . . Chinese and Americans were fighting against the Japanese and the Germans. . . . Therefore, all of a sudden, we became part of the American dream. . . . In the community, we began to feel very good about ourselves. . . . We were so proud [of Chinese Americans] in uniform."
>
> *Harold Liu, of New York City, recalling life in the United States in the 1940s*

thousands more worked in factories building ships and planes and making weapons and supplies. Chinese Americans also bought war bonds to help fund the U.S. war effort. They also sent more than $25 million (about $255 million today) to the Chinese government to help it fight the Japanese.

These developments—along with having a common enemy—helped non-Chinese Americans grow more accepting of Chinese Americans. There was still discrimination, but generally, Chinese Americans felt better treated during World War II than they ever had before.

Postwar Scare

In the early 1950s, the situation for Chinese Americans worsened. The rise of communism in Eastern Europe and parts of Asia after World War II led to widespread anti-communist feelings in the United States. In the midst of the hysteria that arose, a U.S. official in Hong Kong charged that the Chinese communists were sending agents to the U.S. disguised as immigrants. Those agents, he said, would work to overthrow the government. Investigators began questioning Chinese Americans to see if they were loyal and had immigrated legally. This worried many Chinese Americans, including the paper sons who had entered the country illegally. Meanwhile, many Chinese Americans joined anti-communist groups to prove their loyalty.

The CCBA helped relieve the pressure by agreeing with the federal government to what was called the "confession program." Chinese immigrants who had entered the country illegally were encouraged to meet with federal authorities and confess. They would then be investigated and, if the government found they posed no risk to security, allowed to stay legally. About ten thousand Chinese Americans in San Francisco alone—including paper sons—took part in the program and, after investigation, all but 1 percent were allowed to remain in the country.

New Work and Living Patterns

In the 1950s and 1960s, the Chinese American community changed again. For one thing, the older men who had immigrated early in

Citizenship

For many decades, the 1795 Naturalization Act established how foreign-born people could become U.S. citizens. It declared that only "free, white persons" had the right to do so. The 1870 Nationality Act specifically barred people born in China from becoming citizens. That restriction remained unchanged until the 1943 immigration law declared that foreign-born Chinese could be naturalized. This bill applied to more than forty thousand Chinese Americans living in the United States at the time. Few took advantage of the opportunity, however, because the bill put up several obstacles to naturalization. These obstacles were later lifted by the McCarran-Walter Act of 1952. Today, Chinese immigrants are becoming naturalized at a much faster rate than other immigrant groups. From 1991 to 2004, more than 370,000 Chinese-born immigrants became naturalized citizens, behind only Mexican and Filipino immigrants.

Gaining Civil Rights

The postwar world saw Chinese Americans—like other minorities—make gains in civil rights. For years, homeowners, real estate agents, and banks had secretly agreed not to sell homes to Chinese Americans. In 1948, the Supreme Court ruled in *Shelly* v. *Kraemer* that such agreements violated the U.S. Constitution, a decision that helped open the suburbs to Chinese Americans. The Court's 1954 *Brown* v. *Board of Education* decision declared that segregated schools were illegal. This ruling led to the end of separate schools for Chinese American students.

the century were dying. In 1940, the percentage of foreign-born people fell below half of all Chinese Americans for the first time in U.S. history. The community now had more families and more children. By 1960, one-third of all Chinese Americans were under the age of fourteen.

The occupations of Chinese Americans also changed. Veterans of World War II used G.I. Bill benefits to obtain a college education. Armed with degrees, they worked as doctors, teachers, and engineers. By 1960, nearly 20 percent of Chinese Americans worked in professional or technical careers—ten times more than the percentage in 1940. At the same time, the number of workers in sales and service work (like restaurants) had fallen from more than 40 percent to just over 25 percent. These new jobs meant higher incomes, and the average income for Chinese families was higher than the national average.

By this time, Chinatowns were old and cramped, more suitable for large numbers of men living alone than for families. Not interested in living in these conditions, educated professional Chinese Americans did what many other Americans did in the 1950s and 1960s—they moved to the suburbs ringing major cities, where they could find larger, newer homes with yards.

Family Life in the Mid-Twentieth Century

Like other U.S. children, most Chinese American children went to public schools. After the school day ended, however, many went to "Chinese school" where they learned to read and write Chinese and studied the history and culture of China. The older and younger

▲ A group of middle-class Chinese American mothers and their babies socialize in a New York park in 1952.

generations viewed Chinese school differently, with parents insisting that children attend. One U.S.-born Chinese American, however, noted that the children were much more eager to learn in their English-language school and much less interested in Chinese school. Thomas Chinn explained that, "We never thought of ourselves as needing Chinese. After all, weren't we Americans?"

Tension between the generations extended to other areas, such as how girls should behave. "My parents do not believe in freedom of women," one daughter of Chinese immigrants said. She, on the other hand, believed that "a woman should be responsible to no one but herself." Such attitudes clashed with the traditional view of women in Chinese culture. Still, some Chinese American parents did allow their children more freedom.

"In high school, I had never been allowed to go on a date because my parents believed I was too young to consider that sort of thing. So they assumed that when the time was right I would meet the correct Asian guy, and that would be it. . . . The feeling was that when you graduate college and your studies are over, you could concentrate on finding a guy to marry. My parents saw dating as a waste of time, or as an activity that took time away from school work."

Vivian Hom Fentress, the daughter of Chinese immigrants, who married a non-Chinese American man

37

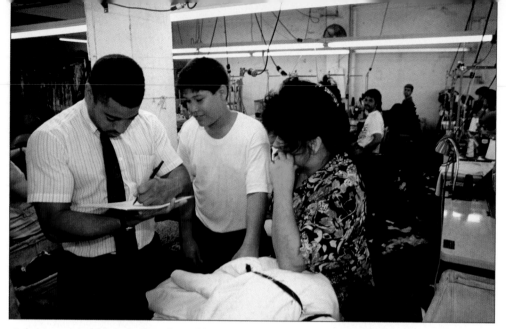

▲ A 13-year-old boy is found working at a sweatshop factory in New York City's Chinatown. These factories have cramped conditions and often hire illegal immigrants.

Another change came in courtship and marriage. Many young Chinese Americans clashed with their parents over dating, with the parents tending to view the practice much less favorably than other U.S. parents. The younger generation, however, generally managed to exert its will when choosing marriage partners. Rather than relying on parents to arrange marriages, young Chinese Americans chose their own spouses.

Families tended to be somewhat larger than among non-Chinese Americans. This trend might reflect the traditional Chinese emphasis on a large family. It might also reflect the value placed on having sons. There was a difference between families formed by immigrants and by U.S.-born Chinese Americans, however, with the latter tending to have fewer children.

The Fourth Wave in the United States

The most recent immigrants—those who came to the United States since 1965—showed some similarities to and some differences from earlier groups. Most of these immigrants came from cities in China rather than rural areas, and many were well educated and skilled. Large numbers, however, were poor and uneducated. These two groups led different lives in their new country.

The poor and untrained tended to work and live in Chinatowns. They labored as cooks, waiters, or dishwashers in restaurants or made clothing in small, cramped factories in these areas. Many worked as many as sixty hours a week and received no overtime pay, health insurance, or other benefits. They were unwilling to complain, however, because the steady flow of new immigrants meant there was always some new arrival willing to take the job. The result was low wages and a life of poverty. These immigrants, immersed in the Chinese community, had little to do with other Americans. In many ways, their lives were similar to those of Chinese Americans in the late 1800s and early 1900s.

Even the highly educated Chinese who came in the fourth wave faced problems. Language barriers blocked some from pursuing the careers they had trained for. Discrimination hurt some who could speak English, keeping their earning power down. Still, many educated immigrants achieved success. They tended to live in suburbs rather than in the cities, many near universities where they taught or research facilities where they did scientific work.

Many brought their own parents from China to live with them. These households looked like the traditional family homes in China, but the relationships among family members made them different.

In the households of Chinese Americans, the elderly parents were living in homes owned by their children, in a country with a culture and customs strange to them. Fathers brought over from China could not dominate family decisions, as they might have in China.

The immigrants of the fourth wave settled mainly in California and New York. New York City became the single most popular place for Chinese Americans to live.

Unlike the sojourners of earlier times, many of these new immigrants were committed to living in the United States. Consequently, recent Chinese immigrants have tended to become naturalized citizens fairly quickly.

▲ A Chinese American graduate student at Harvard University, Cambridge, Massachusetts, during a graduation ceremony.

Chinese Americans in U.S. Society

CHAPTER 6

The 2000 U.S. census showed that more than 2.7 million Chinese Americans lived in the United States. The overwhelming number—98 percent—lived in cities or suburbs. Their population was slightly younger than that of non-Chinese Americans. Reflecting the recent influx of immigrants, about two-thirds were foreign-born.

Family structures illustrated the Chinese emphasis on family. In 2000, only 9 percent of Chinese Americans were separated, widowed, or divorced, compared to 19 percent of non-Chinese Americans. Recent immigrants were much more likely than U.S.-born Chinese Americans to have married another Chinese American.

Chinese Americans had impressive achievements in education. In 2000, nearly 60 percent of those between the ages of twenty-five

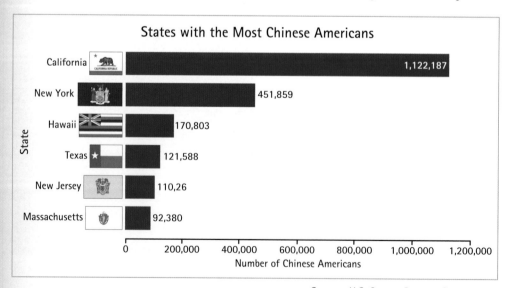

States with the Most Chinese Americans

State	Number of Chinese Americans
California	1,122,187
New York	451,859
Hawaii	170,803
Texas	121,588
New Jersey	110,26
Massachusetts	92,380

Source: U.S. Census Bureau, Census 2000

▲ This chart shows the states where the most Chinese Americans live.

and sixty-four had a college degree, double the rate for non-Chinese Americans. Twenty-six percent of this age group had advanced degrees, compared to only 10 percent of white Americans. Chinese Americans tended to work in managerial, professional, and technical occupations.

More education meant high incomes. The 2000 census showed that Chinese American families had a higher average income than non-Chinese American families. This result is even more remarkable considering that a somewhat higher share of Chinese Americans—11 percent compared to 7 percent—were living below the poverty level. This group of very poor people is made up of the less educated immigrants arriving in the fourth wave.

Growing Acceptance and Ongoing Prejudice

Chinese Americans today enjoy much greater acceptance compared to earlier times. The growing numbers of Chinese Americans in the suburbs interact with other Americans at school, in the workplace, and in stores, and increased contact has lowered barriers between these groups.

Aspects of Chinese culture have gained acceptance as well. Chinese food is the most obvious example, but there are many others. Americans from all backgrounds attend yearly celebrations of Chinese New Year in Chinatowns. Many Americans have begun to study and apply *feng shui*—the use of Chinese principles of balance and harmony—as they decorate their homes. Acupuncture, the ancient Chinese medical practice, has become popular with non-Chinese doctors and patients.

" 'Are you in the Chinese Air Force?' the elegantly dressed lady sitting next to me asked. For a moment I was left speechless. We were at an awards dinner and I was proudly wearing my blue United States Air Force uniform, complete with captain's bars, military insignia, and medals. Her question jarred me and made me realize that even Air Force blue was not enough to reverse her initial presumption that people with yellow skin and Asian features are somehow not Americans. I wish this was just an isolated incident. Unfortunately, too many people today still view Asian Americans as foreigners in America."

Chinese American Ted Lieu, an officer in the U.S. Air Force, writing in the Washington Post *in 1999*

▲ Young Chinese Americans take part in Chinese New Year celebrations in Chinatown, Los Angeles, California.

The Murder of Vincent Chin

In June 1982, Vincent Chin was a twenty-seven-year-old Chinese American studying engineering at a university near Detroit, Michigan. One night, he went with three friends to a bar for a bachelor party. Two white autoworkers were there. They had recently lost their jobs, for which they blamed Japanese car companies. Thinking that Chin was Japanese, they began a fight. Later that night, the two found Chin and beat him to death with a baseball bat. When a local judge gave them a light sentence, Chinese Americans were outraged. In a new trial, in federal court, one of the murderers was sentenced to twenty-five years in prison, although that sentence was later cut short. This incident and other similar crimes have left many Chinese Americans bitter.

Groups of Americans from all walks of life practice *tai chi,* a Chinese form of exercise.

Still, acceptance is not complete, and outbreaks of violence against Chinese Americans still occur. Lingering prejudice is also revealed in complaints about the number of Chinese entering the country. Many Chinese Americans resent the fact that their standing as Americans is doubted.

Even Chinese American gains in education have led to attacks. As the number of Chinese Americans on college campuses increased, nasty signs appeared at some colleges that called these students by vicious names. Ugly incidents of attacks broke out. There have also been reports that some of the nation's best universities began raising their standards for Asian American students, which would reduce their numbers on campus.

Chinese Contributions to U.S. Life

Chinese Americans are not all the same. Some come from families that have been in the United States for more than a century; some have only recently arrived. Some live in Chinatowns that reflect Chinese culture, while others live in suburbs that bear no resemblance to those ethnic communities. Some speak Chinese all the time or at least among family; others speak only English.

Like many immigrants, Chinese immigrants of the fourth wave like some things about U.S. life and are repelled by others. U.S. culture, with its openness and emphasis on the individual, is very different from Chinese culture. Many of today's Chinese immigrants try to maintain Chinese traditions and ways of life at home. Like many others in the United States whose ancestors came to this country long ago, other Chinese Americans see themselves as thoroughly American.

Regardless of their differences, Chinese Americans can look back on many important contributions their community has made to the United States. When they built railroads in the late 1800s, they helped build the nation. When they drained the marshes and swamps of central California, they gave birth to a farming industry that still feeds the country. When they formed social groups to help members of the community, they kept their community alive. When they sacrificed themselves through hard work and long hours, they made it possible for their children to get an education and build a better future.

▲ Practicing tai chi in a New York park.

The Fortune Cookie

Fortune cookies, a popular treat, are not Chinese but Chinese American. No one knows exactly when they were first developed. One story gives the credit to a baker in Los Angeles, while another says they were first made in San Francisco. Either way, the cookie was clearly first developed in the United States, not in China. In 1993, a New York company introduced them to China, promoting the new desert as "Genuine American Fortune Cookies."

Notable Chinese Americans

Joyce Chen (?–1994) Cookbook author and restaurateur who emigrated from China in the late 1940s. She launched a restaurant and wrote cookbooks to popularize the Mandarin style of Chinese cooking. She also started a successful cookware company.

Connie Chung (1946–) Television journalist born in Washington, D.C., to a family that left China in 1945, she became the second woman to anchor a network news broadcast.

Hiram Fong (1906–2004) Lawyer, politician, and businessman born in Honolulu, Hawaii, to parents who arrived in Hawaii in 1872. In 1959, he became the first Chinese American elected U.S. senator, working on immigration issues and the improvement of U.S. relations with China.

Yo-Yo Ma (1955–) One of the world's most highly regarded cellists, known for his excellent technique, beautiful tones, and passionate interpretations of music. He was born in Paris, France, to Chinese parents and came to the United States at the age of seven.

I. M. Pei (1917–) Celebrated architect who was born in China and came to the United States as a teenager. He designed many museums and office buildings around world, including the John Hancock Tower in Boston, Massachusetts, and the Rock and Roll Hall of Fame in Cleveland, Ohio.

Joe Shoong (1879–1961) Businessman born in San Francisco to Chinese immigrant parents. He founded a successful chain of stores popular in California and other western states.

Amy Tan (1952–) Novelist born in Oakland, California. She has written several novels about the life of Chinese Americans, especially women.

An Wang (1920–1990) Technology entrepreneur who arrived in the United States after World War II. He developed several important computer technologies and launched Wang Laboratories.

Wayne Wang (1949–) Film director born in Hong Kong; among his movies are *Chan Is Missing* and *The Joy Luck Club*, based on an Amy Tan novel.

Yung Wing (1828–1912) First Chinese man to graduate from a U.S. college (in 1854). He became a businessman and worked to bring more Chinese students to the United States.

Jerry Yang (1968–) Taiwanese-born immigrant who co-founded the search engine Yahoo!, one of the Internet's most successful companies.

Time Line

1848 Gold is discovered in California, prompting the first wave of Chinese immigration.

1852 The California legislature passes a tax on Chinese-owned gold mines.

1862 The Six Companies form about this time in San Francisco, California.

1865 The Central Pacific Railroad begins using Chinese American workers.

1868 The United States promises to protect Chinese Americans by signing a treaty with China.

1871 In an anti-Chinese riot in Los Angeles, California, whites kill nineteen Chinese Americans.

1882 The Chinese Exclusion Act bars most Chinese immigration; the Six Companies form the Chinese Consolidated Benevolent Association in San Francisco.

1885 In an anti-Chinese riot in Rock Springs, Wyoming, whites kill twenty-eight Chinese Americans.

1888 The Scott Act bars Chinese laborers who leave the United States from returning.

1892 The Geary Act extends the ban on Chinese immigration for ten more years.

1904 The ban on Chinese immigration is extended indefinitely.

1906 San Francisco is stricken by a major earthquake, leading to the entry of Chinese "paper sons."

1910 Angel Island, the immigration station, opens in San Francisco Bay.

1937 Japan invades China.

1941 The United States declares war on Japan in World War II, making the United States and China allies.

1943 The Magnuson Act ends the ban on Chinese immigration, sets low quotas, and allows Chinese immigrants to become naturalized, though only by a difficult process.

1945 The War Brides Act leads to the arrival of about six thousand Chinese-born wives of U.S. servicemen.

1949 Chinese communists gain control of China; opponents flee to Taiwan.

1952 The McCarran-Walter Act makes citizenship more easily available to Chinese immigrants.

1965 A new law expands immigration from China.

1986 A new law allows twenty thousand immigrants each year from both China and Taiwan, plus five thousand from Hong Kong.

1997 Britain hands over control of Hong Kong to China.

2000 U.S. census shows 2.7 million Chinese Americans live in the United States.

Glossary

census official population count

civil war war between two or more opposing groups within a country

clan in Chinese society, a group with the same family name, which includes people who have no direct relation but claim a common ancestor

communist political system in which the government has strong control and property is shared among all citizens

culture language, beliefs, customs, and ways of life shared by a group of people from the same region or nation

delta area formed where the mouth of a river flows into another body of water through many different channels, often marked by marshes and swamps

dialect local version of a language, with its own pronunciation and unique words

discrimination showing preference for one thing over another; racial discrimination occurs when one racial or ethnic group is given preference over another racial or ethnic group

emigrate leave one nation or region to go and live in another place

ethnic group people whose ancestors came from the same country or region, sharing language, culture, and customs

G.I. Bill a law passed in 1944 that gave low-cost housing and college loans to those who had served in the U.S. military during World War II; the law was amended and extended a number of times to include others who had served in the U.S. military

heritage something handed down from previous generations

immigrant person who arrives in a new nation or region to take up residence

naturalization process by which foreign-born people become U.S. citizens

porcelain objects made of clay molded into a shape, baked in high-temperature ovens, and covered with a shiny glaze, a technique developed by the Chinese

prejudice bias against or dislike of a person or group because of race, nationality, or other factors

prospector person who explores an area looking for mineral resources, such as gold or other precious metals, in the hopes of getting rich

quota assigned proportion; in the case of immigration, a limit on the number of immigrants allowed from a particular country

refugee person hoping to leave a country or region because of political conflict, natural disaster, or persecution

ritual set of actions done for religious reasons that must follow a special pattern and that has deep significance

segregated separated on the basis of race or another characteristic

steerage the area inside a steamship where large numbers of poor immigrants lived, ate, and slept during their ocean crossing

stereotype an overly simple image or opinion, usually negative, that people hold of all members of an ethnic, racial, or religious group

Further Resources

Books

Brownlie Bojang, Ali and Barber, Nicola. *Focus on China.* World in Focus (series). World Almanac Library, 2006

Perl, Lila. *To the Golden Mountain: The Story of the Chinese Who Built the Transcontinental Railroad.* Great Journeys (series). Benchmark Books, 2002.

She, Colleen. *A Student's Guide to Chinese American Genealogy.* Oryx American Family Tree (series). Oryx Press, 1996.

Web Sites

Angel Island—Immigration Station
www.angelisland.org/immigr02.html
Web site for Immigration Station Barracks Museum at Angel Island includes text and images recounting the history of the island and Asian immigration.

Becoming American: The Chinese Experience
www.pbs.org/becomingamerican
Web site companion to a PBS documentary includes a time line of Chinese American history, quotations from Chinese Americans, and links to other sites.

Publisher's note to educators and parents: Our editors have carefully reviewed these Web sites to ensure that they are suitable for children. Many Web sites change frequently, however, and we cannot guarantee that a site's future contents will continue to meet our high standards of quality and educational value. Be advised that children should be closely supervised whenever they access the Internet.

Where to Visit

Chinese Historical Society of America
965 Clay Street,
San Francisco, CA 94108
Telephone: (415) 391-1188

Museum of Chinese in the Americas
70 Mulberry Street, 2nd Floor,
New York, NY 10013
Telephone: (212) 619-4785

About the Author

Dale Anderson studied history and literature at Harvard University in Cambridge, Massachusetts. He lives in Newtown, Pennsylvania, where he writes and edits educational books. Anderson has written many books for young people, including a history of Ellis Island, published by World Almanac® Library in its *Landmark Events in American History* series.

Index